The **Black** and White **Club**

'The Black and White Club'
An original concept by Alice Hemming
© Alice Hemming

Illustrated by Kimberley Scott

Published by MAVERICK ARTS PUBLISHING LTD
Studio 3A, City Business Centre, 6 Brighton Road,
Horsham, West Sussex, RH13 5BB
© Maverick Arts Publishing Limited August 2015
+44 (0)1403 256941

A CIP catalogue record for this book is available at the British Library.

ISBN 978-1-84886-179-4

www.maverickbooks.co.uk

This book is rated as: Orange Band
The original picture book text for this story has been modified
by the author to be an early reader.

The Black and White Club

by Alice Hemming

illustrated by Kimberley Scott

It was a quiet evening at the Wildlife Park.

Suddenly, George the giraffe saw some animals creeping past.

"Where are you going?"

George asked his best friend, Sid.

"To the Black and White Club," said Sid.

"That sounds fun," said George.

The penguins ran the club.

"Can I join?" said George.

"No," said the penguins.

"You are not black and white"

But they let Sid in.

All the other animals kept talking

about the club.

George felt sad.

George tried to get in the back door.

It did not work.

He painted himself black and white.

That did not work, either.

George tried to make a club for

giraffes ...but he was the only giraffe.

Then he made the 'Yellow With Brown Spots Club'... but it was a very small club.

So George started the

'Tall and Short Club'.

They wrote a long list of rules.

They made badges.

Everyone wanted to join the club!

The Tall and Short Club

"Can I join?" asked Toni the elephant.

"Yes!" said George.

"Can I join?" asked Minnie the mouse.

"All right, then," said George.

"Can I join?" asked Gus the hippo.

George was not sure.

Gus was not tall or short.

"I'm tall this way," said Gus.

He stretched out his arms very wide.

"OK!" said George.

Mo the flamingo and Max the chimp
were medium-sized.

"Well, I'm taller than him," said Mo.

"And I'm shorter than her," said Max.

"OK!" said George.

"Can I be in two clubs?" asked Sid.

"Of course you can!" said George.

Soon, all the animals at the park joined the club.

The 'Tall and Short Club' was a lot of fun.

Only the penguins did not want to join in.

They liked playing dominoes!

Quiz

1. What is the name of George's best friend?
a) Sam
b) Steve
c) Sid

2. What game do the penguins like playing?
a) Cards
b) Dominoes
c) Chess

3. What size is Toni the Elephant?
a) Medium
b) Big
c) Small

4. What type of animal is Minnie?
a) A mouse
b) A frog
c) A bird

5. Why can't George join the penguins' club?
a) He isn't a penguin
b) He isn't black or white
c) He is too tall

Turn over for answers

Maverick Early Readers

Our early readers have been adapted from the original picture books so that children can make the essential transition from listener to reader.

All of these books have been book banded to the industry standard and edited by a leading educational consultant.

Green

ISBN 978-1-84886-176-3

Orange

ISBN 978-1-84886-179-4

ISBN 978-1-84886-177-0

Turquoise

ISBN 978-1-84886-180-0

ISBN 978-1-84886-178-7

Quiz Answers:
1c, 2b, 3b, 4a, 5b